STEPHEN GAMMELL

HOW ABOUT GOING FOR A RIDE?

Silver Whistle • Harcourt, Inc.
San Diego   New York   London
Printed in Hong Kong

THE BACK SEAT is MINE!

WELL, YOU CAN HAVE iT...

NO FAIR
THROWING CAR
SEATS!

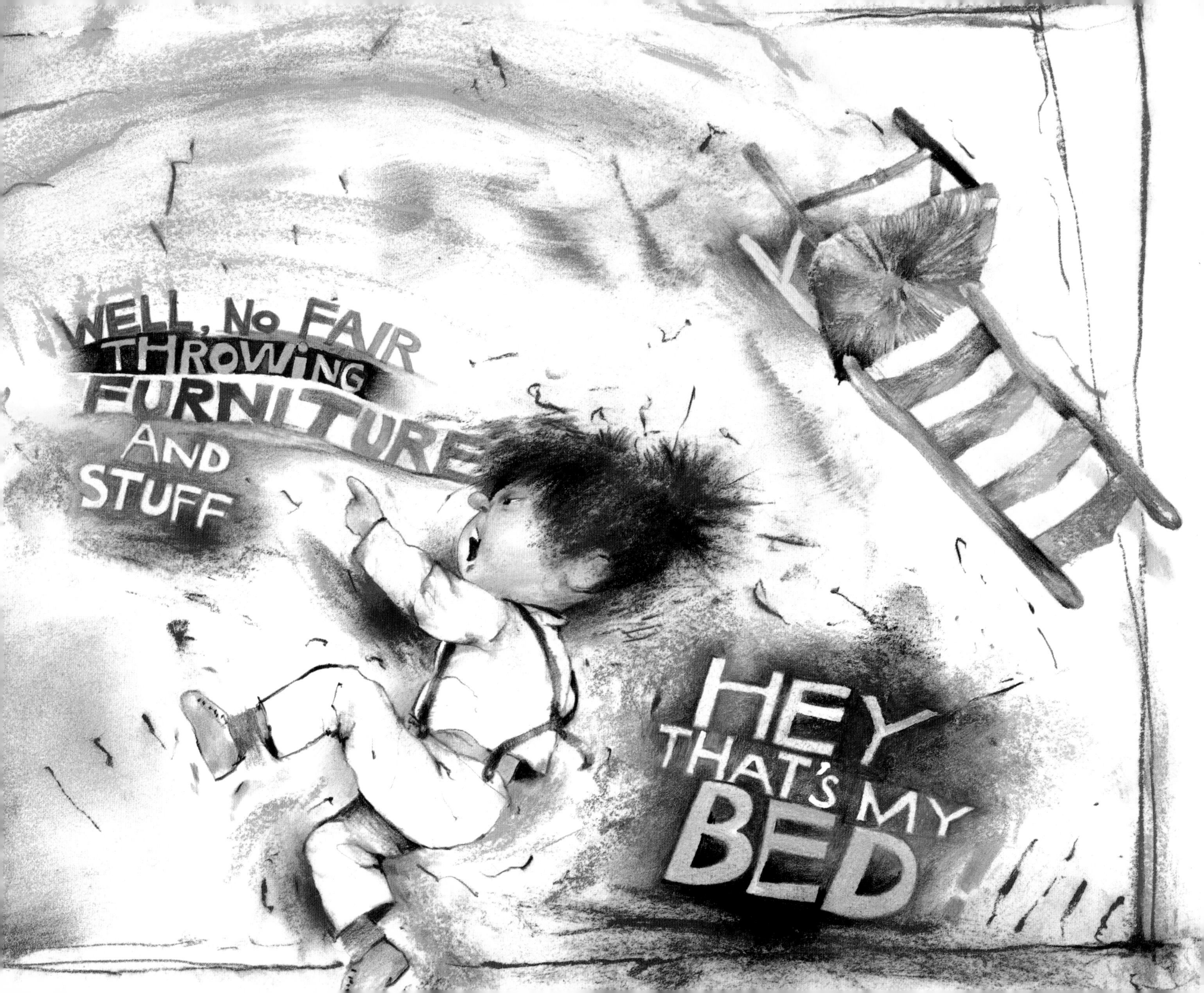
WELL, No FAIR THROWiNG FURNITURE AND STUFF
HEY THAT'S MY BED

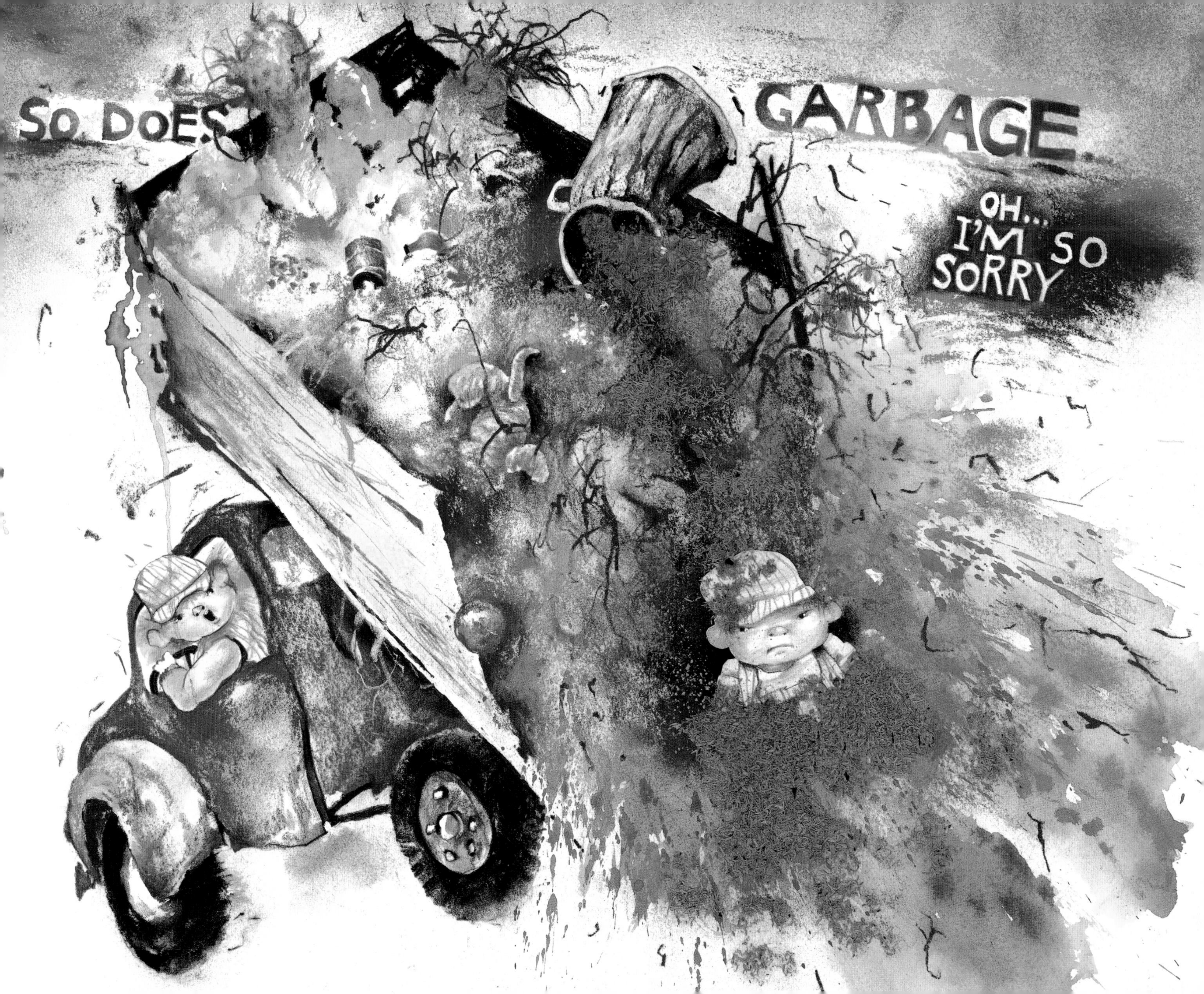
SO DOES
GARBAGE.
OH...
I'M SO
SORRY

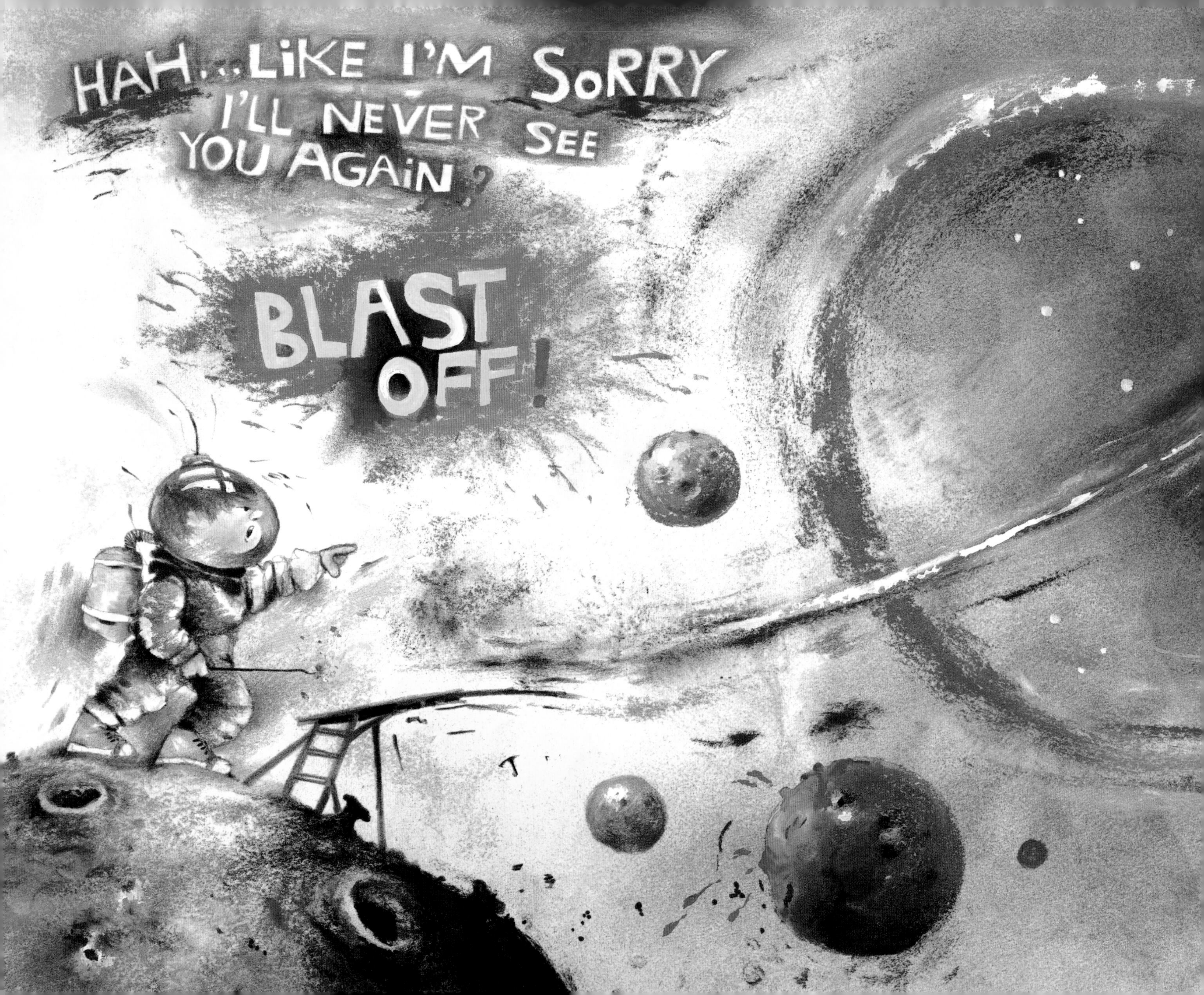
HAH...LIKE I'M SORRY I'LL NEVER SEE YOU AGAIN?
BLAST OFF!

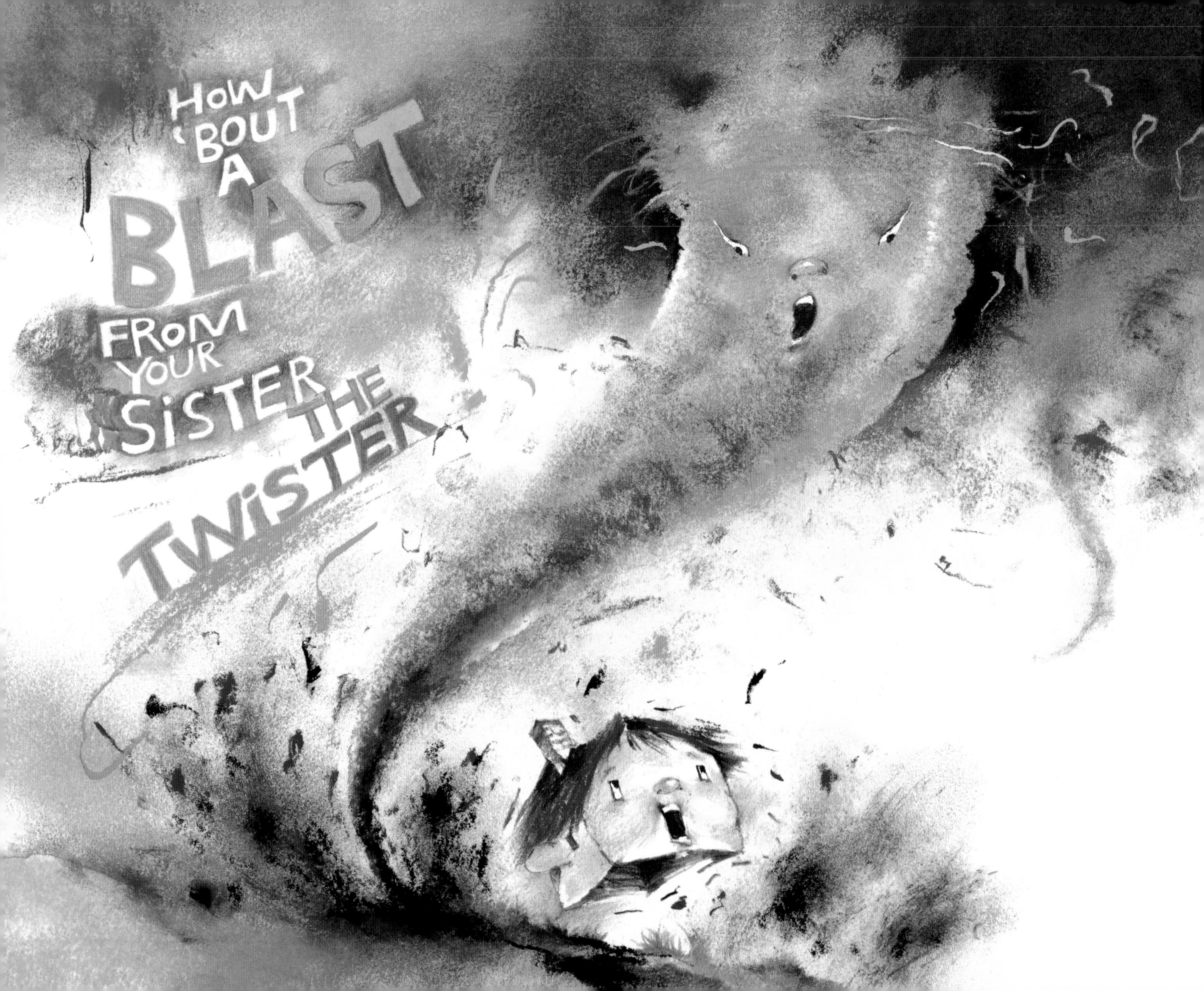
HOW 'BOUT A BLAST FROM YOUR SISTER THE TWISTER

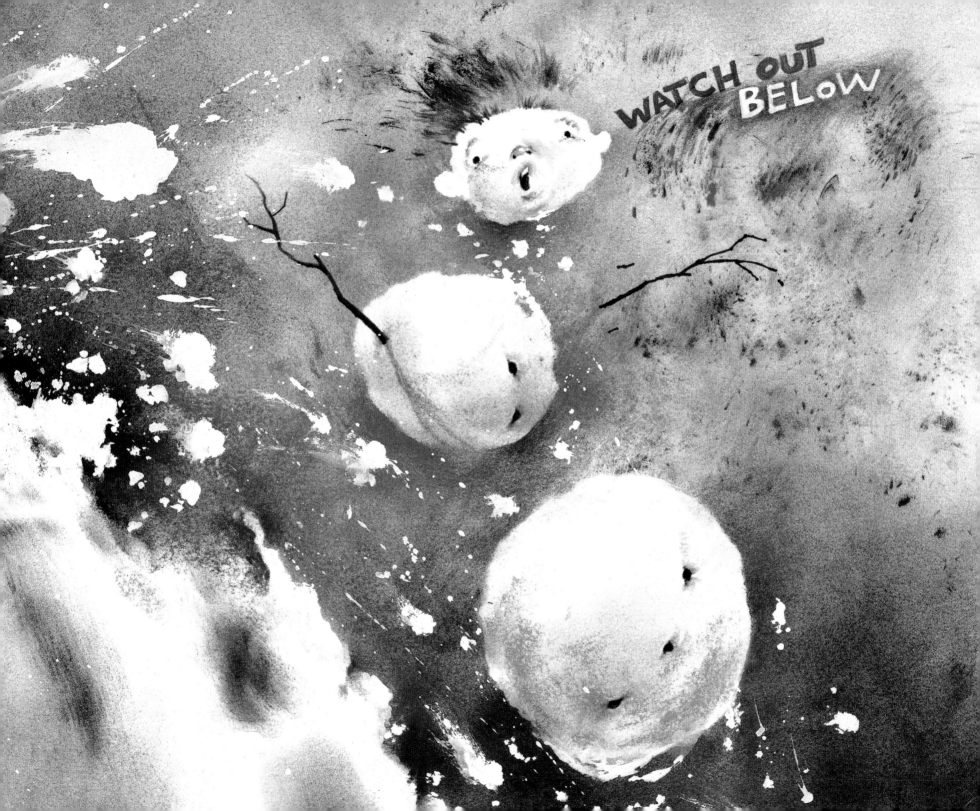

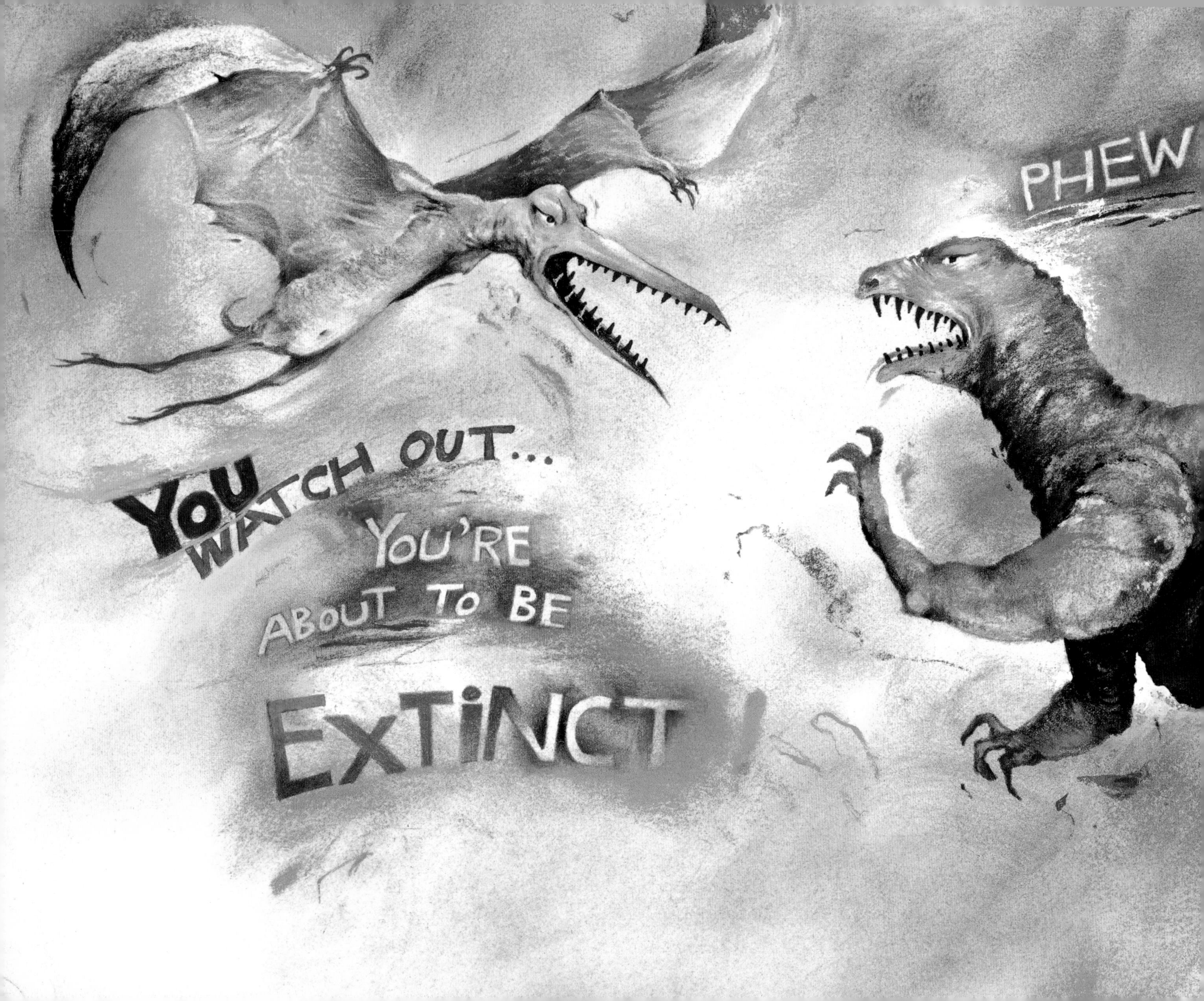
PHEW
YOU WATCH OUT...
YOU'RE ABOUT TO BE
EXTINCT!

GOODNESS
I'LL BET WE'RE
HUNGRY...
WHAT DO WE HAVE?
HARD-BOILED EGGS
AND SOME NUTS...
FRUIT, SANDWICHES...

FoR
BARBARA

LUCAS

Requests for permission to make copies of any part of the work should be mailed to the following address:
Permissions Department, Harcourt, Inc., 6277 Sea Harbor Drive, Orlando, Florida 32887-6777.

www.harcourt.com

Silver Whistle is a trademark of Harcourt, Inc., registered in the United States of America and/or other jurisdictions.

Library of Congress Cataloging-in-Publication Data
Gammell, Stephen. Ride/written and illustrated by Stephen Gammell.
p. cm.   Summary: A brother and sister continually argue during the family's Sunday drive.
[1. Brothers and sisters—Fiction.   2. Automobile travel—Fiction.]   I. Title.   PZ7.G144Ri 2001
[E]—dc21   00-9693
ISBN 0-15-202682-7

First edition   H G F E D C B A

The illustrations in this book were done in pastels and pencils and watercolor on 100 percent rag printmaking paper.
The display and text type were hand-lettered by Stephen Gammell.
Printed by South China Printing Company, Ltd., Hong Kong
This book was printed on totally chlorine-free Nymolla Matte Art paper.
Production supervision by Sandra Grebenar and Ginger Boyer
Designed by Stephen Gammell and Judythe Sieck